CAKE FACE

HARLOW MILLER

This book is a work of fiction. However, the beauty YouTubers mentioned are real people. You're welcome to search them out. All other names, characters, places and incidents are products of the author's imagination or are used fictitiously. Any resemblance to actual events or locales or persons, living or dead, is entirely coincidental.

ISBN-13: 978-1534686359

ISBN-10: 1534686355

To Doug

CAKE FACE

ACKNOWLEDGMENTS

Thank you to my wonderful editors Erin Parker and Maggie Morris for helping me to believe in my story.

Thank you to my wonderful husband Doug for helping me to believe in myself.

1

I woke knowing I'd had a dream, feeling it more than remembering it. After five minutes of trying to get back to the luminous sensation that was evaporating despite my efforts, I gave up and reached for my phone.

I groped around on the pile of décor and fashion magazines that acted as my nightstand until I felt the familiar thin, weighty rectangle of glass and scooped it into my hand. Light hadn't yet started to stream through the dusty blinds into my little studio apartment. The blue glow of my screen flashed on.

It was 6:03 a.m., almost a full hour before I needed to be up. The shrill sound of birds chirping outside gradually dissolved as I became absorbed in the glamour of my Instagram feed. After a few scrolls through images of designer shoes, perfect winged eyeliner and what my friends ate for dinner, I clicked over to what really interested me: the number of views my new video had. The one I'd uploaded last night.

When I saw my YouTube channel page, I bolted upright, suddenly acutely awake. I didn't know how to react. My ears started buzzing, and my throat began to close as I refreshed the screen, swiping down again and again. When nothing changed, I restarted my phone and padded across the creaky hardwood floor to the small desk by the window so I could check from my laptop. It simply couldn't be right.

8,998,967 subscribers.

When I'd turned the lights out last night, I had 303.

2

My heart was beating so loudly I could barely concentrate. There was no reasonable explanation for it. Nothing had gone viral. I was not trending for telling a terrible joke on Twitter, thank goodness. I was still, as far as I knew, not Beyoncé. There'd clearly been a mistake. There must have been some kind of glitch in the system that had worked in my favor—to put it mildly.

I checked the views on all my videos. My "How to Choose a Foundation Color Online" video had suddenly and mysteriously jumped to 354,867 views, up from 184 last night. My "Holy Grail Eye Shadows" and "Best Lipsticks for Medium Skin Tones" videos were racing each other to 500,000 views. My "Five Perfumes for People Who Hate Perfume" video was lagging at only 280,443 views, still an astronomical number by my newbie-YouTuber standards.

I wasn't sure what to do. *What is one supposed to do when one inexplicably receives nine million subscribers to one's beauty channel overnight, exactly?* I wasn't a "career" YouTuber like many of the beauty gurus I subscribed to. I was Ashley Thoms. I wasn't Tanya Burr, the adorable Brit who parlayed her three million subscribers into her own cosmetics brand, an autobiographical lifestyle book and the cover of *Glamour* magazine. I could never be Jaclyn Hill, the hysterically funny, fast-talking, former MAC store employee who was now making a living from her ballooning beauty channel while doing massively-popular collaborations with makeup brands on the side. I was not Michelle freaking Phan, the YouTube beauty titan turned mogul who was now part owner of a subscription beauty service valued at over $800 million, a multichannel video network slash music label, and—you guessed it—her own cosmetic line.

The point is, I had not paid my dues. I hadn't been doing videos since the early days of YouTube when people filmed on their laptops, and no one had ever heard of a ring light. I had not been building my channel for years, a few subscribers at a time, like most successful YouTubers had. I had a day job. I was just a girl with a new hobby.

Caffeine. I need caffeine.

3

I felt a little off kilter and sweaty when I finally got up and shuffled the five feet from my desk to my micro kitchen. The plant I'd given an emergency watering to the night before was now looking enthusiastic and full of promise. I touched its leaves with jittery hands, empathizing with how it felt.

I had launched my YouTube channel about three months ago in a fit of decisiveness, forcing myself to press Record after almost a year of dithering and hesitation.

I'm an introvert, but if you knew me only by my YouTube videos, that fact would likely be a surprise to you. On camera, my slightly crazy, kind of outrageous, overly talkative side takes over, and I say things I wouldn't dream of saying if another actual person were in the room with me. It's as if I achieve the perfect state of inebriation the second the Record button is pressed.

I quickly washed my favorite mug, noticed that my slate-gray manicure was holding up well and made a mental note to add the topcoat I used to my monthly favorites.

As you'd expect from someone who starts a beauty channel, makeup is my jam. Everything about it gives me the tingles and the joys. Raiding my mother's makeup cabinet was one of my favorite pastimes when I was eight or nine, and it continued to be until I was finally allowed to wear my own, sometime around thirteen. I remember scandalously sneaking into my parents' ensuite bathroom when they weren't home, opening the medicine cabinet, taking no notice then of the Valium and painkillers that I now know were there, and instead keenly running my fingers across my mother's taupe eye shadow and plummy cream blush. I suppose I should be grateful that my addiction today is to shimmer and not pills.

I'd been watching YouTube beauty videos since back in the day when there were only a few women uploading regularly. Back when the concept of *beauty gurus*—that is, makeup-loving women who apply cosmetics on camera and discuss the products they use with their viewers—was so new that beauty brands hadn't even heard of them yet.

I remember binge watching Michelle Phan's slightly blurry, dreamy-voiced videos when I first discovered them in 2008. Panacea81, aka Lauren Luke, a single mother from South Shields England, was the beauty phenom at the time. I was fifteen when a mere one million views of her "Leona Lewis

Bleeding Love Inspired Makeup Look" video was enough to prompt news crews to camp out on her doorstep and for the BBC to make her the subject of a documentary. I was seventeen when her "By Lauren Luke" makeup palettes launched at Sephora, and Lauren found herself swarmed by fans when she appeared at the Times Square store in New York. She was a pioneer, and I was fascinated.

But it was the growing makeup community itself that really compelled me. This swelling group of women, girls and men all over the world who shared the one interest of mine that none of my real-life friends or family did. I'd grown up in a family of doctors and professors, serious people for whom makeup was not worthy of much thought, much less an obsession. Women in my family were known to amateurishly apply mascara and, as they called it, *rouge* only on special occasions.

The new online community of women I'd discovered made me feel something I didn't often feel in my day-to-day life. They made me feel *normal*. A small but unrelenting voice inside pestered me to connect with them. I brushed it off for months, but it eventually wore me down.

I uploaded a test video one fateful afternoon after a dramatic inner battle in which my shyness was narrowly defeated. Mercifully, the first comment I received was so encouraging and sweet that I was forever hooked. Considering my tissue-thin skin at the time, if that first comment had been from a hateful troll, I might never have continued. *Bella1281, I'll always be grateful.*

I called my channel "The New Ash," in honor of the new self I felt I was on the verge of becoming. That and the fact that coming up with a channel name was very stressful, and "The Ash Bash" was already taken.

In only three months, I'd recorded more videos than many YouTubers do in a year, sometimes uploading as many as ten in a week. I discovered that not only did I love filming and editing, but I also loved the feeling of being helpful. I gave useful information that I wanted as a viewer but couldn't find elsewhere; I provided matter-of-fact reviews of products I'd bought; I made color and texture comparisons that would help me if I were researching a product, and I created easy-to-follow, diverse tutorials. I was effusive about the products I loved and snarky about the ones I didn't. And, in addition, because I adored and was schooled in design, choosing type, colors and effects in the editing process was a big part of the fun for me. The whole process gave me the creative outlet that my job as a plebe in a design studio didn't afford me—one that I sorely needed.

I leaned my iPhone up against the chipped, white-tile backsplash beside my prized espresso maker and picked a video from my YouTube feed to play while I made coffee.

"Ooh, a new Kathleen Lights. Sweet," I said under my

breath and tapped her video immediately. Kathleen, a hilarious and loveable Miami-based YouTuber, was quickly becoming one of my favorites.

My phone pinged with a message sent to my YouTube email, and my jumpy nerves sent coffee grounds skittering across the counter. I paused Kathleen, unintentionally freezing her in an awkward, eyes-half-closed, mouth-open pose. With a sense of foreboding doom, I opened Gmail.

To my utter relief, it wasn't a letter from YouTube confiscating all my new subscribers as I'd been fully expecting. Instead, it was an email from someone named Arielle Prenger from the brand Make Up For Ever.

I unclenched.

When the contents of the email finally sank in, my heart began pounding rambunctiously all over again.

4

Dear Ashley,

I just discovered your channel, and I love it!

I'd like to send you a set of our Ultra HD Concealers for potential review. I hope you love them as much as we do! Please let me know your mailing address.

Kind regards,
Arielle Prenger
PR Director, Make Up For Ever

Oh my god, it was happening. My makeup-addict's dream was coming true. I was being sent high-end makeup. For *free*.

I turned twenty-three this year and have a typical "first job out of college" salary, which is to say I can see the poverty line from here. My makeup budget is on the paltry side, to put it mildly. I can't afford any frosted-glassed, velvet-pouched, magnetic-capped department store makeup without sacrificing something from the important column, such as food, rent or wine. But like most other makeup junkies, I am prepared to eat an awful lot of Manager's Special peanut butter on brown toast to be able to afford a decent Sephora haul.

And as most new beauty YouTubers do, I've often fantasized about growing my channel to the point where makeup brands would take notice and start sending me their beautiful new collections to test. It had seemed so out of reach even a week ago.

But what if Make Up For Ever finds out about the mistake? What if they find out these aren't really my subscribers? That I'm not the YouTube beauty unicorn they think I am? I was suddenly awash in feelings of inadequacy. Only this time, that all-too-familiar sensation was based in fact; I didn't just feel like a fraud. I actually was one.

Another ping.

Hi Ashley,

My name is Hadas, and I work for Burberry.

We love your channel and would like to offer you a set of products from our new spring makeup collection to try and enjoy. We would ask you to please share and review it on your channel.

We'd also like to give you a set of Burberry Kisses Lipsticks in the new spring colors to use as a giveaway for your subscribers if you wish. Let us know what you think of the idea.

Best,
Hadas Blum,
Burberry

Oh god. It was so happening.

5

I paced the length of my tiny kitchen as my phone began to ping incessantly. Sunlight was now splashing across my white, still-unadorned walls, letting me know that I was going to be late for work. I placed my feet inside each of the black-and-white tiles with each step I took. It helped me think.

How on earth am I going respond to these offers? My hands trembled as I checked my channel for the hundredth time. Thankfully, all the subscribers were still there. In fact, I'd gained another two hundred in the last half hour.

I read email after email from brands big and small, old and new, all gushing about their new launches, new palettes, new formulas and new colors. I couldn't help but be particularly enthralled by the offers from the luxury brands; I wanted so badly to write back and say, "Sure, send all your gorgeous goodies my way. I'd be happy to review them." Of course I'd leave out the fact that I've never actually had the guts to approach any of those impossibly intimidating high-end makeup counters, much less shell out $60 for a highlighter. My hot, prickly anxiety returned.

Okay, calm down. What's the big deal if I let them send some makeup to me? It's not actually a lie that I have 8,999,167 subscribers as of right now. I don't know how I got them, but I do actually have them. Even if they disappear tomorrow, there would be no actual deception if I accepted the products right now, I argued with myself, fairly convincingly.

It was true. All the makeup brands wanted was exposure. And I could give it to them as far as I knew. *This is not that big a deal. This is merely a business transaction*, I thought, trying to suppress the elation—or was that greed?—bubbling up inside me.

I decided that if all "my" subscribers were still there when I got back from work, I'd accept the brands' offers.

And so, when I returned to my apartment that day to 708 new subscribers, goosing my total to 8,999,875, I lost the argument with myself. Or perhaps more accurately, I won.

6

As I crafted and sent brief replies to the emails I'd received that day, I felt my cheeks flush with excitement. An entire Burberry spring makeup collection, with its silky, luxurious finishes and shiny, gunmetal packaging, was on its way to me. I would finally get to experience the eye shadows and blushes so many people raved about on YouTube. I tucked my fists under my chin and freestyled a giddy, new, "living the dream" dance.

"This is soooo okay, totally fine," I said aloud as I considered what to do next, my hips gradually jerking and swaying to a stop.

I went to my computer and, in a woozy, Zen-like trance, began adding my mailing address to the description box of all my videos.

Then the obvious thought finally occurred to me. *I should make a video.*

Instantly driven, I began setting up my camera in front of the window where I usually film. I went through my mental checklist for filming as I pulled out my small, desktop tripod. *Natural light, check. Minimal street noise, check. Guy upstairs not lumbering and thumping about, check.*

My apartment is in one of those older, walk-up buildings with terrazzo in the stairwells, arched doorways, years' worth of thick paint on the windowsills, and doorknobs that have "character." It's on a somewhat leafy, one-way residential street, just off a newly trendy main street with several *it* restaurants where I can only afford appetizers. My street is usually pretty quiet, even on a Friday afternoon like today. The bartender who lives above me was either at work already or asleep and about to miss work, based on the absence of his heavy footsteps. It was an opportunity to film a video if there ever was one.

"Right. What am I filming . . . ?" I mumbled as I checked my notebook for ideas. I tried not to think too hard about how all those new subscribers were going to react when a new video from me popped into their feed.

"Adele tutorial for hooded eyes" was scrawled on my ideas page. I really look nothing like Adele, but I love her trademark makeup look. My skin tone and hair color are a bit darker than hers; my eyes don't have that deep crease I've always longed for and I have a long, sharp nose (I've managed to inherit the "challenging" features of both my German father and Chinese mother). This video would take some prep work: finding the perfect matte-black liquid eyeliner and choosing the right light-toned under-eye concealer, contour powder, and rosy-nude lip color for my skin tone. It would also require shooting photos where I'd mimic one of Adele's poses in an attempt to look at least somewhat like her to give the tutorial some credibility.

Too. Much. Trouble.

I needed something I could film impulsively, right now.

"Drugstore Dupes" was the next practically illegible scrawl. I was excited to do this video since I'm a frugal girl, both out of necessity and as a result of watching my mom go miles out of her way just to pay a few cents less for milk "out of principle" when I was growing up. Getting a good deal is a thrill that's hardwired in my family, so finding a $5 lipstick that looks and feels the same as a $30 tube fills me with more joy than it realistically should. This video was a definite must-do, but with all the new press samples on their way to me, I decided to wait to see if there were any dupes to be found in that bounty.

"GRWM" was the next scribble on the list. A "Get Ready with Me" video immediately seemed like a good idea and a realistic one for my mood. I wanted to be impulsive and unstructured, which GRWM videos, with their "I just turned on my camera—let's chat while I put on my makeup" ethos, could accommodate. Plus I'd promised Chels I'd have a drink with her in a couple of hours and needed to get ready anyway. I'd just be doing it on camera.

It was settled.

7

I put my alarmingly large number of subscribers out of my head and pressed Record.

After twenty-four minutes and twenty-three seconds of reapplying concealer, blending it out with a damp sponge, defining my upper lash line, highlighting the inner corners of my eyes and lining my waterline while I ranted about a recent customer service experience (*sales assistants who hate your jobs, please do us all a favor and quit*), I said goodbye. I gave my usual two-fingered, peace-sign wave.

I checked my watch, and with more than an hour and a half before I had to leave, I clicked open iMovie and started editing.

I didn't have the luxury of time to nerd out on type and effects the way I normally would, so I kept the editing inventive but minimal. I chose a dreamy atmospheric track to cut to and, for fun, added some jarring hip-hop at the end. I was well practiced at editing by now, so I worked quickly and made choices with my gut. Before long, I was ready for the next step.

Nerves fluttered in my stomach as I clicked the Upload button. I avoided looking at my subscription counter as I dragged my GRWM video file onto the page.

I sat riveted as the upload bar filled with blue horizontal lines and began inching across the screen. After several minutes, a bathroom break and a scroll through Twitter, the upload was complete. I added the title "Chatty GRWM | Friday Night," filled the description box with the products I'd used and checked my watch again.

My heart started thumping as I moved my cursor onto the Publish button. I felt blood rush into my head and pound against my eardrums. I placed my thumb on the track pad, and, with what felt like bravery under the circumstances, applied just enough pressure to make that familiar, muffled *thap*.

Soon, nine million people around the world would be notified of what I'd just done.

8

I checked my phone to see how long it would take for the video to appear in my feed. Nothing. Nothing. And there it was.

A text came in from Chels.

Running a bit late, it said. This was not news.

No probs. Let me know, I wrote.

I love Chels, but she hasn't been on time once since I've known her. It was as if her birth three weeks past her due date signaled that lateness was a part of her genetic code. I had to stage an intervention last year in a desperate plea for advance notice of when and how late she was going to be at any given time. This text—believe me—was progress.

By the time I went back to YouTube to check on my video, it had 10,298 views. *Um. Whuuut?* Up until this morning, it had taken months for one of my videos to reach 1,000 views. One of my *popular* videos.

I started reading some of the comments with trepidation. For a naturally shy person, it's never easy to expose myself, and uploading a new video always feels like jumping off a cliff.

Love this look. You slay, commented Grumpy Lara.

So freaking pretty, said Jacee Bajana.

Amazing!! I love your personality, Ash, said TessaC.

A rush of excitement and love for these women came over me. *Yup, this is why I adore YouTube.*

My phone vibrated.

On my way now! texted Chels.

Comment after comment rolled in, totaling 313 already. As I backed away from my computer, the video had 11,155 views.

Eleven thousand one hundred and fifty-five views. In nine minutes.

I can't deny that this experience was incredibly seductive. It made me feel loved and understood, even though those numbers meant neither of those things. Mostly, it made me feel I wasn't alone in my obsession with makeup—a hobby I had a hard time talking about in public.

I put on my leather jacket and quickly wrapped a lavender and gray infinity scarf around my neck. I put on my tan suede booties and rolled my jeans up just enough that a little bit of ankle was showing. A little bit more. No, a little less. No, a tiny bit more. The "effortless look" I was going for was definitely not effort-*free*.

Be there in 5, I texted as I finally walked out into the hallway and locked my apartment door.

As I swung the strap of my bag across my body and slid my phone into the side pocket, I debated whether to tell Chels the secret I'd been keeping from her all these months.

9

Chels isn't my oldest friend, but she's my closest. We met at the graphic design studio where I still work today; she was a junior art director, and I was a junior designer. She's everything that I'm not: hip, athletic, extroverted and blonde with long, corkscrew curls, making her instantly attractive to most guys. She's also completely unsure of who she is and who she wants to be, which makes her far less intimidating to be around than she would be otherwise. We hit it off right away.

Despite our closeness, I've never told Chels about my YouTube channel. I have no excuse; I don't really know why I've never mentioned it. I take that back. Of course I know why. It's the same reason I haven't told anyone else—not a single friend, family member, coworker or even random acquaintance: I'm terrified of being judged.

Yes, I'm that girl, unfortunately. I'm anxious that if people close to me knew about my makeup obsession, they'd think less of me. I know my parents would. I'm apprehensive of anyone knowing how much makeup I actually own (too much by any sane standard) and then figuring out how much I spent on it (a troubling amount). I'm nervous about letting people who don't love makeup themselves see how much I lust after highlighters and eye shadow palettes and that I actually *collect* them, of all things. It's not as if I'm collecting eighteenth-century coins or first-edition books. I'm well aware that my interest in contour powder doesn't exactly project a literate and worldly mind-set.

Are you judging me for worrying so much about other people judging me? I wouldn't blame you.

But when I finally uploaded that first video months ago, I realized two things: one, no one is watching what I do as closely as I think they are; and, two, no one *really* cares what interests me. While those two facts are slightly depressing on one hand, they are exactly what set me free on the other.

* * *

I pushed open the oversized matte-black doors leading to the crowded hotel bar with slight trepidation. Chels was always suggesting relentlessly stylish places like this, where only the popular kids from high school seemed to be allowed in. But despite perpetually feeling like an imposter at the places we met, I never complained, opting instead to soak up the cutting-edge décor that was so inspiring to my enthusiastic, design-thirsty eyes.

I walked into the grand space and drank it all in. The sitting areas were visually defined by several oversized white columns and giant vintage letterforms snatched from the tops of old buildings. Oversized leather library couches faced velvet lounge chairs, and were separated by low, oiled-wood coffee tables. The ornate ceiling was painted black and the antique lamps encircling each of the white columns bathed all the plaid-shirted hipster patrons in warm, flattering low light. Small library tables with iconic green desk lamps dotted the space with irony.

I saw Chels sitting at a corner table by the bar, her piles of blonde curls drawing the eye like a Chanel bag in a thrift store. I greeted her with a high-pitched, melodic "haaaa-ay" and a warm hug, as I always do.

Before we'd even slid into our chairs, she looked me in the eye and blurted out what she'd obviously been stewing over for some time.

"Ryan sent me a dick pic, but it was addressed to someone named Anna," she said, bursting into tears.

"What?" I exclaimed, suppressing a knee-jerk laugh. Seeing that Chels was on the verge of an ugly cry, I set aside the delicious scandal of what she'd just told me and focused on my distraught friend.

"Hey. Don't worry, sweetie. This could happen to anyone," I said, handing her my cocktail napkin. "If he'd do this to you, he's not worth your tears."

I was secretly relieved to have the emergency role of supportive friend to play. It meant I wouldn't be telling Chels about the miraculous thing that had happened to me that morning. An adulterous dick pic sent by a boyfriend of nearly two years clearly trumped my news and would take all evening to parse. My secret YouTube channel would stay just that.

After walking Chels home and reassuring her that Ryan's dick was better off in Anna and that I'd be there for her no matter what, I briskly hiked the block and a half from her building to mine.

I smiled to myself as I jogged up the three flights of stairs to my apartment, pleased that I'd been able to comfort Chels. As I made my way to my door at the end of the hallway, I found myself marveling at the fact that I finally had a place of my own, still not quite over it. Living with roommates, as I had up until six months ago, would still be more prudent on my salary, but the extra financial pain was definitely worth it.

I unlocked the door and made a beeline to my computer, throwing my coat and bag on my favorite flea-market-find chair on the way. When I saw the numbers on the screen, my mouth went dry.

224,580 views. 2,417 comments. 24,698 thumbs-up. 58 thumbs-down.

Um. Whoa.

10

No matter how hard I tried, I could not seem to adapt to my new normal. Twenty days had gone by and my heart still raced every time I saw the astonishingly high number of views each of my videos now had. The near full-time job of replying to the comments that flooded in every time I posted a video was starting to interfere with my *actual* full-time job.

But even though I was still pleasantly aghast at the fact that I now had well over nine million subscribers, the gnawing fear that it would all disappear as quickly as it had come was always with me. How would I feel if my "Best Beauty Products Under $10" video, that now had 1,189,664 views, went back to the 204 views it had before?

Let's face it. This was my dream. It's every YouTuber's dream, isn't it?

I went to my walk-in closet—or claustrophobic bedroom, if

I chose to stuff my bed in there as others in the building had—and grabbed my pair of lavender Converse. It was time for my new favorite thing to do in life: visit my PO box.

Passing my full-length mirror on the way out, I decided to braid my fine (read flat), dark brown hair into pigtails. *Better.* I slipped my nearly pristine, vintage Coach bag across my body and casually slid on the pair of Dita cat-eye sunglasses I was still paying off (I don't want to talk about it).

After taking a quick OOTD selfie for Instagram, I strode past the collection of empty boxes left over from my last trip to the post office. All the spent cardboard and bubble wrap still reminded me of the lusty thrill of opening each package every time I walked past. I felt a little rush as I stepped out the door.

I skipped down the stairs wondering what fabulous creams, glosses, powders and polishes would greet me today. Grinning idiotically, I leaned into the well-worn metal handle of my building's front door and burst out into the warm spring air.

I was, however, in no way prepared for what was waiting for me at the post office when I got there.

11

I opened the white, 5" x 8" envelope from Google without once inhaling. Nervously, I unfolded the paper inside. At the top, I read the computer-generated, all-caps type slowly to myself. "This check is for your earnings as part of the Google AdSense program."

My eyes traveled in slow motion to the green check at the bottom. I read my name. Then I read the number.

$10,789.45.

It was more money than I'd ever seen on a check before. In fact, it looked like a joke check to me. Something my brother would mock up on the computer and include with an unfunny note in a birthday card.

This was more cash than I'd ever personally possessed. But the obvious question still gnawed at me: What would happen if and when someone discovered how this had all come about?

Now that there was money involved, was I stealing? Would I go to jail if I cashed it? I took a quick, deep breath and tried to will my brow into an un-furrowed state.

If I deposit it but don't use the money, I could at least make some interest. Surely that's not illegal. I felt no certainty whatsoever.

Then it occurred to me. No matter how I ended up with the subscribers I had, this check was based on the number of views my videos were getting. *That part of this insane situation is actually legit.* Within moments I went from tormented to jubilant.

I stuffed the check in my purse and noticed the unprecedented lack of lineup at the counter. I hurried over to take advantage. After being motioned over, I slid my fistful of package notices to the bored-looking woman opposite me. Wordlessly, she pushed her mousey hair behind her ears and took the slips with her to the back. When she returned a few minutes later, she was holding a laundry basket-sized tub full of brown cardboard packages.

"Is it your berrr-thday?" she asked in an Aussie lilt when she saw my face light up at the sight of them.

"Sort of," I said cryptically, noticing her naturally ruddy cheeks and the fact that she wasn't wearing a stitch of makeup. She likely didn't have a clue what a beauty vlogger was or that a huge community of makeup-obsessed women existed on the Internet.

She shrugged with her lips in response, pushed a pile of acceptance forms in front of me and pointed to the *X*. I signed for my mountain of boxes and thanked her as I placed package after package into the giant blue-and-yellow IKEA shopping bag I had brought along in anticipation. There were so many different shaped boxes that fitting them all into the bag was a puzzle that took several attempts to solve.

A man who looked younger than his white hair and outdated gray suit implied held the door open for me as I waddled out of the post office, my unwieldy bag in tow.

"You're my hero," I said as I passed him. He gave a soft chuckle in reply.

Once outside, I slung the straps of the bag over my shoulder and kept to the edge of the sidewalk in an effort to avoid taking out oncoming pedestrians. My thoughts drifted back to my uncertain situation, and my brow crept into the furrow that was rapidly becoming its default state. I'm a typically sunny person, and this constant state of low-grade worry was starting to wear me down. I'd had enough.

Within three blocks, I'd made a decision: I would stop preparing for the worst. *If I'm going to live in this dream world, I might as well enjoy it.*

I stopped at my bank, deposited the check and stared at the balance on my phone the entire way home.

12

I was barely through the door to my apartment before I tore into the first box, breaking the tape with a mechanical pencil that was lying in my cluttered entryway.

Inside, I found a dozen small matte-black boxes with the familiar white lettering that I'd coveted for years. I shook the nude, pink and red lipsticks from their boxes in my favorite Cremesheen and Lustre finishes and swirled my ring finger into a bronzy, metallic eye shadow from one of the three limited-edition palettes in front of me. I opened one of the Mineralized Skinfinishes but didn't dare touch the pearly surface, knowing how collectible they were and how much others like these often went for on eBay. Hundreds of dollars worth of MAC makeup, all free. I glanced at the beautifully printed promotional pictures and dropped them back in the cardboard box.

I was giddy with excitement and gratefulness. MAC had always been a brand that I lusted after, striking the perfect balance of aspiration and inspiration for me: their products were just out of reach price-wise, often housed in tantalizing, limited-edition packaging, and every new collection was full of shades that were just ever-so-slightly different from the ones I already owned. The makeup universe had expanded so much since the early days of YouTube when MAC was the be-all and end-all, but I still had a soft spot for them—one that was downright squishy.

Along with the kid-in-a-candy-store elation I was feeling, however, came a sensation that took me completely by surprise: pressure. Surely MAC now expected me to make a video giving the collection a favorable review, as would Burberry, Benefit and the rest. *Did I owe it to them in return for this bounty? Was the gratefulness I was feeling a double-edged sword?*

I began to understand why typically genuine YouTubers often gave strangely insincere new product reviews.

My phone pinged. The emails from makeup brands hadn't stopped coming in. Every new email offered something more generous than the next, and each lavish overture was now making me feel increasingly queasy. Of the two hundred or so new messages I was now receiving each day, most were from brands, some were from PR companies or agencies acting as middlemen for brands, and some were petrifying invitations to attend events and speak on panels. "Would I like to be a keynote speaker?" *No, I most certainly would not.*

A few video networks—companies that assist YouTubers in growing their channels and brand sponsorships in exchange for a percentage of earnings—were also starting to sniff around and offer their services. It was all a bit overwhelming.

But the new email at the top of my inbox was different from the others. I didn't know it at the time, but it would change my life forever.

13

I clicked on the email from Sloane Smythe.

Dear Ashley,

I'd like to offer my warmest congratulations on reaching nine million subscribers. This must be a very exciting time for you.

I am launching a new brand of luxury cosmetics, and I would love to discuss an opportunity with you. Would you be available in the next week to meet with my branding team and me?

Sloane Smythe,
CEO, Sloane Smythe Cosmetics

I was intrigued and panic-stricken in equal measure. You would think that a personal note from the CEO of a new high-end makeup brand offering a mysterious opportunity would, at the very least, provoke curiosity. But instead, it instilled terror. My ridiculous, debilitating, shame-inducing shyness had taken the reins and was very much in charge. A meeting? Couldn't they just email me the info? It was one thing to accept products by mail, but it was entirely another to meet and potentially have to lie in person to a *team* of people.

> *Hi Sloane,*
>
> *Thank you for getting in touch! Your opportunity sounds intriguing. My calendar is very busy over the next while—would it be possible for you to send the info over email?*
>
> *Best,*
> *Ashley*

It was worth a shot. The response came almost immediately.

> *Hi Ashley,*
>
> *I'd prefer the opportunity to meet with you in person so we can show you the range and discuss the possibilities of*

working together. We believe it would be worth your while.
Let me know what availability you have, and we will try
to work with your schedule.

Regards,
Sloane

She'd seen right through me and was clearly an "I don't take no for an answer" type of woman. I admired her already. And, as I've learned from past experience, crippling fear tends to go hand in hand with admiration. I'm a "get pushed around by pretty much everyone" kind of girl, myself.

A quick Google search only made Sloane Smythe more intimidating. She appeared to be in her late forties, had strong, classically beautiful features, fashionably choppy straw-blonde hair, and had won many prestigious industry awards for makeup in the past. She was on the board of several charities and had apparently made millions when she sold her stake in her friend's yoga-wear company.

I agreed to a meeting at her office the next day.

14

I woke up at 6:00 a.m. the next morning with an anxious knot in my stomach. Lying on a futon in my little studio apartment, staring at the bumpy, peeling layers of paint around my windows while imagining walking into a sleek boardroom to sit across from Sloane Smythe and her "branding team" was already making my palms sweat. Clearly I was going to be a wreck by the time the meeting started at 8:00 a.m. (I had suggested the ungodly hour, figuring that I could go to the meeting and still make it into work by a reasonable 9:15 a.m.)

I showered and nervously attempted to dress myself but found that I was completely incapable of making a wardrobe decision. *What on earth do you wear to a meeting like this anyway?* My gut was saying, *Something professional and put together*, but I didn't own much in that category. After an energetic purge a couple of months ago, I now owned only one fitted charcoal "presentation blazer" and one pair of black dress pants that look good on me but make me feel like I'm trying to be someone else.

I decided to go with a pair of black skinny jeans instead, paired with a long, flowy, blush-colored top and the charcoal blazer with the sleeves rolled up. Once I'd added a navel-length gold necklace with a triangle-shaped pendant, the look felt put together but still casual enough that people at work wouldn't accuse me of coming from a job interview.

I went for a glowy "New York Fashion Week" look for my makeup. According to all the blogs, the *it* look this year was dewy skin with a classic flick of black liquid eyeliner, mascara and a hint of sheer color on the lips. I found a video interview with Olivia Munn sitting in the front row of one of the shows looking all glowy and flicky and paused it for inspiration. When I finished, my makeup looked natural but intentional—not trying too hard. *Perfect*.

By now my nerves had really started to kick in. My heart was pounding in its usual obnoxious way.

"This should count as cardio," I said to my reflection.

I was used to getting nervous before presentations at work, but at least I knew what I had to say in those few-and-far-between situations. The idea of "just meeting with" accomplished, glamorous, rich strangers without knowing what I had to do or say was paralyzing me with fear. I would have nothing to hide behind; there would be nothing but myself to show. And I had no reason to trust that I wouldn't completely embarrass myself; I'm reasonably smart, but my brain has the tendency to freeze up when I'm talking to people I'm intimidated by. I'm also terrible at small talk, so I tend to be quiet and come across as socially awkward. What can I say? My few strengths lie elsewhere.

"Maybe I can fake the flu or something," I suggested to myself in a panic. Based on how nauseous I was starting to feel, it might not actually be a lie.

As the clock on my phone ticked closer to 7:15 a.m., I decided to have a word with myself.

"Stop being a child," I told myself firmly. "They contacted you. They have to impress you," I said, taking myself by the scruff of the neck.

I took a deep breath and did my best to exhale my worries.

"You can do this," I said tightly and stepped out the door.

15

I arrived at the address I was given in the up-and-coming part of town. I looked up to see an older, yellow-brick building with glass doors rimmed with dark green, almost-black paint.

I was a few minutes early, as I am to everything. I stepped into the vintage elevator and pulled the metal accordion gate closed. When it gave a secure-sounding *clunk*, I pushed the button for the top floor and looked up as the machinery whirred and clanked.

"Breathe. Just breathe," I told myself.

When the elevator door opened, I walked out into a plain hallway with white walls and gray industrial carpet. There was only one door, about five steps to my right, on the entire floor. The small stainless-steel plaque beside the frosted-glass entryway said Sloane Smythe Cosmetics in small, tasteful type. I turned the handle and pushed.

The office was in a converted loft with refurbished honey-colored hardwood floors and walls extending up to the exposed pipes and ductwork on the ceiling, all painted the same shade of creamy white. The dark machinery stains spotting the floors betrayed the space's origins as a garment factory. Small, raised, brushed-silver letters formed the words *Sloane Smythe Cosmetics* and sat elegantly on the matte-black, angled wall that faced the entrance. A small sitting area was made up of '60s era white vinyl and chrome chairs with a low, glass-topped coffee table between them.

"Can I help you?" asked a raspy voice to my left. I turned to face the most beautiful trans woman I'd ever seen. She was sitting behind a half wall that screened the reception desk and appeared to be in her early forties with long dark hair and completely poreless, glass-like skin. Her large, perfectly-manicured hands were folded casually in front of her on the desk, and her dark, lashy eyes were smiling just as much as her nude, glossy lips. I liked her immediately.

"I'm here to meet with Sloane Smythe?" I said in a quivering, high-pitched voice.

"You must be Ashley. She's expecting you. Have a seat," she said reassuringly.

I chose the closest white-vinyl chair and sat down apprehensively. An artful display of current fashion magazines sat atop the coffee table that, I was pretty sure, cost more than two months of my rent, conservatively. I grabbed the latest *Vogue* to give myself something to focus on. I was barely past the table of contents before I heard a voice behind me.

"Ashley?" said a woman with a throaty mid-Atlantic accent.

I jumped up a little too quickly.

"Yes, I'm Ashley," I said to the tall blonde woman behind me. It was Sloane Smythe in the flesh, and she looked even more striking than I was prepared for. Unlike the photos online, she now had a supersleek boy cut but with a drape of platinum, chin-length hair shading part of her left eye. She wore a Helmut Lang asymmetrical cream silk top, cropped skinny dress pants and suede high-top sneakers.

Great. This woman in her late forties was hipper than I was.

"Lovely to meet you, Ashley. I'm Sloane. Thank you for agreeing to meet with us. I know you're very busy," she said in a staccato fashion as she led me past the half wall that separated the reception area and the rest of the office. Many of the spacious desks were still empty this early in the morning.

"Oh, my pleasure," I said sheepishly. "I love this space," I offered, trying to change the subject.

"Right, thank you. We just moved in last month. We tried to keep the renovation modest, you know?" she said as she led me around the corner to a very immodest glass boardroom where three stylish people sat around a long, bleached-wood table. The place was dripping with Isabel Marant and Alexander Wang. I clutched my H&M vegan bag uneasily. All three turned to face us as we entered the room.

"Guys, this is Ashley."

They each got up and shook my hand one by one. They had warm smiles and cold hands, thanks to the air conditioning that was strangely on full blast for such a cool morning.

"This is Jen, our social media coordinator," Sloane said as she gestured to the small yet somehow willowy Korean girl across the table from me. She was around my age with shoulder-length light brown hair and pastel-pink ombré ends. Her makeup was flawless, and her brows were Instagram-perfect. "So nice to meet you. You're so pretty in person," she said sweetly. Something about the lack of force in her voice made me feel at ease.

Sloane gestured to the thirty-something woman beside Jen. "This is Samantha, my marketing director."

"Call me Sam," she said, smiling but not looking me in the eye. She had chin-length blonde hair with more than two inches of intentional dark roots. I recognized her Isabel Marant blazer from one of the websites I often stalk recreationally. *Hashtag, outfit goals.* Her eyes ever-so-quickly scanned me up and down.

"I'm Jason," said the man next to her.

"Jason's our creative director," Sloane interjected.

He had dark wavy hair, gray eyes and a long handsome face with a bit of stubble concealing, but not hiding, the dimple in his chin. Around twenty-seven was my guess. He wore an expensive-looking gray T-shirt, a heavy silver watch and dark jeans. When he stood up and offered his hand, I noticed that he wasn't tall, maybe 5'9", was fit and had beautiful forearms.

"Nice to meet you," I said, looking away quickly, trying not to ogle.

On the table in front of us were some of the most incredibly packaged makeup products I'd ever seen. The sleek, matte-silver cases had the look of melted metal. The heavy, unique shapes had a sculptural feel, more like jewelry than packaging. The eye shadow quads in front of me were in colors that were all up my alley and in unique combinations: warm coppers, plummy browns, rosy nudes and shimmery golds. Each shadow was embossed with the letters *ss* and had a pristine sheen, indicating that they'd never been touched.

"Go ahead," Sam motioned, encouraging me to swatch and play with the products. I obliged, grateful to have something to do other than look awkward. Phrases like *high-density pigments, skin-care ingredients, luxury textures* and *runway-inspired colors* were thrown around while I dipped my fingers into the creamy, mousse-like powders.

"Riiight. Shall we?" said Sloane abruptly after a few minutes, bringing the meeting to a brusque beginning.

"So, Ashley, we've been watching your channel, and we're all very impressed," she squinted as she spoke, giving her words a strange overemphasis. "I find your approach very real and authentic. There's an emotional magic that comes across with you." She moved her small hands in a way that resembled karate. "The more we watched you, the more we fell in love with you." Her icy blue eyes bored into me, making her compliment feel invasive. Despite this, I blushed at the idea of Jason watching my videos.

"We're going to be launching my line next month, and we'd like to partner with you to get the word out," Sloane said with a smile that didn't reach her eyes, making her warm words seem strangely hollow.

"Our plan is to partner with three different women," Jason said, jumping in, "one with fair skin, one with medium-toned skin and one with dark skin, and to have each share with her viewers the colors in the collection that best flatter her. You'd be our medium-toned partner." His relaxed demeanor deflated the tension left over from when Sloane spoke. His voice was resonant, but his delivery was soft and confident. His eyes, directed toward me, were thrilling. I nodded and tried to look professional.

"So, what do you mean when you say 'partner,'" I quietly asked the room, hoping this wasn't a stupid question.

Sam responded this time.

"We'll give you the full line of products and a marketing calendar of videos we want you to make. You'd start with swatch videos of all the colors in your range for each of the products. Then you'd do 'Look-Book' videos once a week, and both a 'Favorite Products' video and a giveaway at the end of the month—see here?" She pointed to the calendar. "You would link to our online store in every video, and you'll earn 9 percent commission on sales," she said, looking me in the eye for the first time, making sure I registered this point. "That's a percentage point higher than the affiliate commission Charlotte Tilbury offers bloggers," she said, widening her eyes for emphasis. "A lot of other brands only offer a flat fee for a video. Because we're offering a commission, your incentive is the same as ours. The more your video sells, the happier everyone is, including you. The more videos you do, the more money you make," she said, sliding a price list across the table.

Sloane did the math for me. "Your videos are averaging about 800,000 views each. A typical sale conversion rate is .01 percent, so that's 8,000 on one video. For 8,000 sales of our $45 illuminator, your commission would be $32,400." If your video is very convincing, the conversion could be as high as 5 percent, which would make your commission $162,000.

I swallowed audibly. Who knows what my face was doing. I had no control. I was lucky I could still control my bowels.

I looked at all the gorgeous highlighters, blushes,

foundations, eye shadow palettes, primers, eyeliners, contour palettes, brow pencils, lip pencils and mascaras on the table in front of me. I glanced at the price list Sam gave me. Even with my feeble math skills, I could see that a video for each of these products had the potential to be very lucrative. As far as I could tell, I was going to be filthy, stinking rich.

I don't really remember what was said after that. I remember seeing people's mouths move, and I'm sure words came out of them, but I really couldn't tell you what they were. I was drugged by the knowledge that I was about to make hundreds of thousands of dollars.

I giddily signed the papers Sloane put in front of me and left the meeting feeling like the luckiest person alive.

16

By the time I got to work downtown, the studio was in full swing, and there were emergencies already waiting for me. The client hadn't approved a layout, and if the changes weren't made ASAP, we'd miss the printing deadline. Our usually unflappable studio manager, Leslie, was having a quiet yet agitated conversation in the corner with Mateo, the head designer. I looked over at my coworkers, Siobhan and Julia, who were stoically staring at their computer screens, wisely ignoring the drama unfolding in the corner.

I dropped my bag, put my head down and got to work. But as hard as I tried to put the morning's meeting out of my mind, I found it almost impossible to concentrate. The idea of being paid $24,000 a year to create final artwork for flyers and design promotional emails for irritable clients who practically dictated the layouts suddenly felt a bit grim.

I decided to walk home after work; I've always been able to think more clearly while walking. I slipped out of the office at exactly 5:01 p.m.

I ran down the five flights of newly carpeted but rickety-sounding stairs. When I burst outside, I realized how much I'd been craving fresh air. Though, considering our office was located on a busy, exhaust-choked thoroughfare, *fresh* was perhaps a relative term.

I snaked up a side street and turned left onto the main shopping street, marked in my mind by the potent homemade soap smell wafting from the LUSH store on the corner.

I walked quickly past shops that would normally catch my eye. Even ZARA's new Coachella-inspired window couldn't distract me from everything that was swirling in my head.

Today marked exactly three weeks since the morning I'd woken up to find that my YouTube subscriber total had changed and, along with it, my life.

I was gradually starting to realize what having one of the largest beauty channels on YouTube really meant. It was becoming clear to me that my new and rather sudden status as a "big beauty guru" didn't just mean free stuff and a check from Google every month.

It meant power.

I was walking even more quickly now. I glanced at the L'Oréal billboard on top of the building at the corner ahead and the clusters of women pouring in and out of the shops underneath it.

I had what the beauty industry wanted: the ears and eyes of millions of women and girls who were interested in makeup. What had dropped in my lap three weeks ago wasn't just nine million new friends to talk to—it was a thriving business.

I decided to start taking my new business seriously. I'd have to get organized. No more filming whenever I felt like it or had time. My fickle schedule of ten videos one week and none the next would have to go. I'd start filming regularly and on specific days every week. And if I didn't want my channel to look like the Sloane Smythe Cosmetics channel, I'd have to plan on doing plenty of videos in addition to the ones I was now obligated to do.

I turned off the main shopping street onto a run-down side street and strode toward the entrance of the park at the end of the road. When I reached it, I felt a blip of euphoria as the green, leafy openness replaced the miles of cracked concrete. I took the worn path of dry, unyielding earth beside the tennis courts as my mind raced.

I would plan my videos ahead of time so I would know the mix of topics in advance. This way, videos requiring a lot of prep like "dupe" videos could be spaced out between less time-consuming ones.

I'd need all the requisite equipment of a serious YouTuber:

a ring light and a decent camera so I didn't have to rely on bright daylight to film. I'd also need to buy some better video-editing software and maybe even consider moving to a bigger apartment—something larger than my current one-room space so I could avoid tripping over my filming paraphernalia on my way to the bathroom at night.

I took the park path out onto another busy, though less touristy, street. I was in Little Portugal now, and the luscious smell from the Portuguese Churrasco chicken restaurant I was passing made my mouth water. I forged on, knowing I still had a very big decision to make.

I would have to consider quitting my job to make time for all this work.

But what if this all goes away tomorrow? I deflated slightly as I always did whenever this nagging and annoyingly valid question popped into my head.

I decided to put it to rest once and for all.

17

Dear YouTube Support,

I received a lot of subscribers all at once recently and just want to confirm that my account in the YouTube Partner Program is in good standing. Please let me know if the new subscribers were a mistake as I am considering quitting my job and investing in equipment for my channel.

Thank you,
Ashley Thoms

I decided to come clean. If there was going to be a problem, I wanted to know about it. Even if it meant leading them to the problem, knowing was better than living in purgatory. I was not up for standing at this fork in the road forever.

I pushed away from the computer and did my best to occupy myself the rest of the evening.

I cobbled together a dinner of sorts—some leftover dim sum from the weekend and a few baby carrots that I ate out of the bag—while I watched the vlogs of a self-absorbed LA girl I love to hate until I couldn't stand it any longer. I tried everything I could think of to distract myself from the fact that I was about to be handed either the biggest disappointment or the biggest gift of my life. I tried reading a book, but I wasn't retaining a single word and had to keep rereading the same page. I tried watching Netflix but was so indecisive I managed to spend an entire hour scrolling through options. It was as if my brain was so full of the day's drama it was actively resisting any more in any form.

Finally, I gave up and went to bed—and spent the entire night staring at either the ceiling or my phone.

* * *

The next day at work, every mundane client change seemed to irritate me more than usual. Either the lack of sleep and overabundance of caffeine in my system was making me ornery, or the sudden dwarfing of my salary by Sloane Smythe's offer was the culprit. I shook my head at the memory of the figures she'd thrown my way only yesterday.

An email from someone I didn't know appeared in my inbox. I froze when I realized what this could be. I held my breath and clicked it open.

Dear Ashley,

Thank you very much for contacting YouTube Support. Congratulations on your new subscribers.

I closed my eyes for a moment. If this was bad news, I wanted to stay oblivious for just a moment longer. Curiosity forced them open again.

We have reviewed your account, and all appears to be in order. We can confirm that your account is in good standing. Feel free to invest in your channel.

Best regards,
Matt Assimakopoulos
Account Manager
YouTube Partner Program

I let out a yelp of laughter. I knew it wasn't a guarantee, but it still felt like a thousand-pound weight had been lifted. I felt dizzy with relief.

That's about as much confirmation as I'm going to get that the sky isn't going to fall, I told myself. Everything that was happening and that could happen was officially real now.

I sent a meeting request to the head of my department for tomorrow afternoon. It took surprisingly less hand-wringing than I thought it would to start the process of quitting my job of fourteen and a half months.

I have $10,000 in the bank. If this all goes to shit, I'll just get another job, I told myself and typed "best ring light" into my search bar.

18

It was past 6:00 p.m., and I was cross-legged on my bed in the midst of drafting my new content calendar when my phone rang. This was alarming, mainly because my phone never rings. I'm a text-only kind of girl.

I looked at my screen. "*Call from Jason Caruso.*"

My eyes widened as the electronic xylophone of my ringtone bore down on me. Panicking, but seeing no other option, I held my breath and allowed myself to be pulled over the falls. I touched the green receiver symbol.

"Hello?" I said. I was going for casual and sultry but only managed to sound groggy.

"Hi, Ashley? It's Jason. I met you yesterday morning at Sloane Smythe's office," he stated unnecessarily. My heart sank a little at how professional he sounded.

"Hi, Jason. How can I help you?" I said coolly and crisply.

Two could play at this "professional" game.

"Well, I was wondering if you'd like to meet to go over the styling for your videos. I thought we could go for a drink and talk about it," he said with what sounded like a smile.

I could feel my heart jostling my rib cage. "Um, sure. That sounds good. When were you thinking?" I asked as casually as I could muster.

"How about tonight? There's a restaurant near here that has a nice wine list. Do you know the Mockingbird?" he asked smoothly. Even the sound of his voice was too good-looking for me.

I agreed to meet him in an hour. *At Mockingbird Bistro, bitches!* The one voted "Best Date Restaurant" the past three years running. *Jason* wants to meet *me* at a well-known, unapologetic "date restaurant"! The elation I was feeling didn't stop me from breaking out in a cold sweat, however. This man was completely out of my league, and I wasn't sure if I would be able to form sentences in front of him.

I quickly looked up a "Date-Night Makeup Look" video from Pixiwoo (a channel by two talented British makeup artists who happen to be sisters) that I'd mentally filed. I watched it studiously while I changed into my favorite pair of jeans and a loose, black V-neck top that's technically low cut but has a lacing detail that says "fashion" more than "cleavage."

I adapted the Pixiwoo look to my features, added a gleamy

highlight to my eyes and applied a flattering shade of lipstick that I knew wore like iron.

"Well," I said to my reflection, "this is as good as it's going to get."

I ordered an Uber.

19

Entering parties and restaurants alone always gave me an unwelcome twinge of anxiety. I got out of the car and girded myself as I walked toward the bustling patio with the red awning and French bistro chairs.

I forced my lips into a subtle smile to soften my resting bitch face, walked into the restaurant and quickly swept my eyes around the room.

Inside, tattooed waiters wearing crisp white aprons glided past me. The cozy room glowed with warm light, absorbed by the ornate chestnut-colored wood bar, and the exposed-brick wall in the back. The warmth and patina of the well-worn room put me at ease.

I spied Jason, who had snagged the prized booth at the end the bar. His eyebrows were raised adorably, and his fingers waved just below his dimpled chin. I smiled and walked toward him, willing myself not to trip.

He got up to greet me and leaned in for an air kiss. I obliged and slid into the booth, proud of not screwing that up.

"I'm glad you could come," he said with what felt like a twinkle in his eye.

"Me too," I said, feeling the need to avert my eyes but unable to look away.

The waiter arrived at our table and placed a beer in front of Jason.

"India pale ale," he announced casually. "And what can I get you?" he asked, turning to me.

I was relieved Jason was having a beer. "A glass of your house red, please," I said without looking away from Jason. We held each other's gaze for what felt like an eternity. I was utterly unable to tear my eyes from his face.

He broke the spell by glancing at the door. "Ah, there's Sam," he said, waving her over.

Not quite believing what he'd just said, I looked at the door. And, indeed, there she was, phone in hand and Balenciaga handbag in tow. Seeing us, she made her way toward our booth.

"Ugh, sorry I'm late, so crazy," she said, rolling her eyes and squeezing in beside Jason. I wanted to disappear. I hid my humiliation as best I could.

She ordered a martini with three olives and some bruschetta

because she was "staaaarving."

We spent the next hour talking about lighting and the best way to shoot close-ups of all the products. We talked about appropriate typefaces and whether I wanted assistance with any of the filming. I graciously declined, carefully failing to mention that I can only truly be myself if no one else is in the room.

They offered a studio set and then talked themselves out of it. Best if the look of my videos stayed consistent, they concluded, and I agreed.

We said our goodbyes after we had drained our drinks. Jason hailed a cab for me and held the door open while I got in. I avoided his eyes the entire time.

"Thanks," I said, looking at my feet with as much of a smile as I could muster. The slam of the door put a period at the end of my so-called date.

As the cab lurched forward, my guard finally came down and I relaxed into the stinging rejection I'd been trying to hide all evening. I watched couples on the busy street though the window as we drove by, and I unsuccessfully tried to bat away the sensation that was so achingly familiar: the feeling that I'm not enough.

20

The next few weeks went by in a blur.

I quit my job, which I still couldn't quite believe. Very quickly, the decision felt right and not only gave me an incredible sense of rebirth but also seemed to heighten a parallel feeling that I was finally in control of my destiny. Of course that didn't stop me from also experiencing a good dose of unexpected remorse—and anxiety that I'm an idiot. The roller coaster is *real*.

My boss surprised me by offering me a raise to stay on. It was to $30,000 a year, which would have thrilled me not too long ago but, with recent developments, seemed too measly to consider seriously now. I was touched nonetheless. I told her I was quitting to start my own business, so if it didn't work out, she would be the first person I'd contact. I meant it, and we agreed to stay in touch.

My going-away party was a lesson in how much I was actually going to miss my coworkers. There were so many funny, smart people in the studio, and I was giving up a lot of laughter. Not to mention a place to go every day.

I hugged Mateo, the sweet Argentinian head designer who called us all angels and often regaled us with stories about his sex life.

I hugged each of "the girls," Siobhan and Julia, who were my coffee confidantes and trusted sources of Kardashian intel.

I hugged Leslie, the übercapable and underappreciated assistant studio manager with the athletic gait and acerbic wit, who we all looked up to and admired.

I even hugged Vlad, the competent but insular new guy, whom none of us really knew anything about.

I would miss all of them more than I knew. Because as much as I dismissed my job as "crap" and "mind-numbing" to my friends, I secretly liked it. And, in hindsight, I loved the people more than I realized.

But as soon as that part of my day-to-day existence came to an end, my life suddenly took on a sublime newness. Even the most mundane tasks took on a fresh, optimistic sheen. My morning walk through my neighborhood to Starbucks no longer felt routine and repetitive but, instead, buoyant and hopeful. The fact that it was often 9:30 a.m. by the time I made the stroll, much later than when I used to have to be at work, filled me with a euphoric feeling of independence. I was a bouncing bundle of self-reliance and the electricity of being at the precipice of something exciting.

I'd decided to keep my little apartment for the time being. I liked my neighborhood and, even though it was tiny, my apartment was what most people would call "a find"; despite its age (or perhaps because of it) it had character, big windows, a decent-sized bathroom and that pièce de résistance, the walk-in closet. Plus, all my videos to date had been shot there, making it a consistent backdrop, which felt important. I'd just have to deal with the fact that all my fancy new filming equipment was always going to be somewhat in the way. I'd figure it out. First-world problems.

I threw myself into my channel. I soon had a three-month calendar of videos planned out in meticulous detail. I spent mornings replying to comments and letters from incredibly sweet subscribers, responding to emails from brands, posting on social media and doing any prep work necessary for shooting. I was filming new videos in the afternoons, three times a week, and planned on upping that schedule to four with the Sloane Smythe launch next week.

But along with feeling an enormous sense of forward motion and excitement about the future, I was also beginning to experience something exceedingly unwelcome and strange.

I was starting to become numb to all my new makeup.

Every time I went to the post office, I would return with such an overwhelming quantity of press samples that I often didn't open all the boxes. *Me. Not opening boxes full of makeup.*

Somehow, it seemed that receiving entire collections of makeup, free of charge, just wasn't the same as spending hours researching, pining for and finally shelling out for a few select pieces.

Was this new development related to the pressure I was beginning to steep in with every new box? Admittedly, "Press Sample for Review" was starting to read to me like "We expect a video in return for this, and there'd better be gushing." I tend to be conscientious and considerate by nature, which for the first time in my life seemed to be working against me.

Did all beauty gurus feel this way? Was I the only one?

I had a hard time reconciling my general euphoria with this bizarre cocktail of numbness and obligation. I tried to dismiss it as a consequence of my channel doing well, but something about it ate at me. I felt as if I was switching sides. No longer was I an ally of my viewers, giving them ideas and helping them navigate the sea of beauty products; I was joining the side of the beauty industry with my viewers in the crosshairs.

I found myself unexpectedly veering toward cynicism for the future of YouTube and the beauty industry's role in it—a rabbit hole of pessimism I was fighting tooth and nail to stay out of. I didn't want to feel this way. My channel was going to the moon. This so-called business of mine was a huge success. Now was not a good time for a crisis of conscience.

If only I could go back to the way I felt when I opened those first boxes just a few weeks ago.

I told myself I was just having a down day. *I just need to go for a walk and shake this off.* Closing my laptop, I threw on some trainers and my military jacket, stuffed my phone in my pocket and headed out the door.

21

I decided to kill two birds with one stone and do some shopping for dinner. I took the long way to the grocery store for some visual stimulation and the possibility of spontaneous recreational shopping.

I stopped at Belfry Books, my favorite used bookshop in the city. They always had a great selection of new titles, even though they were a second-hand shop, and their art section rivaled those of many art gallery bookshops. It was around the corner from my apartment and was one of the real reasons I was reluctant to move. I walked into the large, low-ceilinged, intimate space, eager to see how the selection had changed since the last time I was there. The smell of paper, leather and floor wax hit me the second I walked in, giving me a Pavlovian feeling of comfort and excitement thanks to my bookish upbringing. I went to the New In section and gradually made my way around the corner to the cookbooks as I usually did, nodding to the clerk, the only other person in the store. I scanned the titles, hoping to scoop something from my Amazon wish list for a fraction of the price.

I heard the bell on the door ring as someone walked in. I glanced around the corner, always curious who made up the clientele of this store. I nearly hit the deck when I saw who it was.

Jason.

I looked down and nonchalantly slid behind the Sci-Fi shelves. I was still smarting from what had happened the last time I saw him and didn't know if I was capable of making small talk. I moved out of his sight line as he followed a similar path to mine near the entrance. I picked up a book and pretended to read as I watched him through the wire racks.

Jason scanned the New In section quickly and then walked over to Crime Fiction on the other side of the store. I watched as he picked up a trade paperback copy of Truman Capote's *In Cold Blood* and thumbed through it, seeming to consider purchasing it. He put it back though and started moving in the direction of the architecture section. And me.

Panicky, I jammed the book I was pretending to read into the rack and turned away from him, moving farther inside the store. I found a section that felt hidden from the rest of the shop, slid in and decided to camp out there.

I kept my eye on Jason as best I could through the wire racks. He continued on from Architecture to Film, casually making his way to the back, wandering closer and closer. *Goddammit.*

I grabbed a book off the shelf and buried my head in it, trying to hide my face without being obvious. Unfortunately my attempt to conceal my rather large head with a small paperback failed miserably.

"Ashley?" said Jason, smiling.

I feigned disorientation and surprise.

"Oh, Jason. Hi! I didn't see you!" I said, motioning to the book.

He nodded with an odd smile on his face, his eyebrows raised. "Is it good?" he asked.

I looked down at the cover. In my hand was a dog-eared volume of *The Best New Erotica 12.* A quick look around confirmed my fear: I was standing in the Erotic Fiction section. My face grew hot.

"Pfff, you didn't think I was . . ." I trailed off, laughing, and tried to slip past him into the Literature section. "It was on the floor. I was just picking it up for them," I said, now feigning helpfulness. I could feel his smiling eyes following me.

"Oh, I see. So what *do* you like to read then?" he said, scratching his chin playfully.

I looked down at the display table beside us and saw one of

my old favorites. "This one's great," I said as I picked up a faded copy of *High Fidelity* by Nick Hornby.

"A classic!" he said in a cute, excited way. "I loved that one. Nick Hornby's great." His eyes scanned the table. "Have you read this one?" he asked, picking up *Sharp Objects* by Gillian Flynn.

"Not yet," I said, a little excited myself, "I've been meaning to. I loved *Gone Girl.*"

"Me too," he said, "but this one's better." It felt like there was a current running from his gray eyes to mine.

He led me around to some books and authors I hadn't heard of, an adorable smile always on the verge of his lips. I had to try Ned Beauman, Michel Faber and Haruki Murakami, he told me. We stood closer and closer to each other with each recommendation, and he began touching my arm when he remembered a book I had to read. I looked over at the store clerk, who was sneaking glances at us over his book. It felt as if there were a magnet between Jason and me, drawing us closer and holding us in position. Had I read the short story that *Brokeback Mountain* was based on by Annie Proulx? he wanted to know.

"I have—it's fantastic," I told him, and even though my hips were nearly touching his, I couldn't move away. I was stuck in his orbit by his damn gray eyes. I touched his arm to show him a book that I'd read over and over again, but he didn't look down. His eyes were on me, and they didn't move.

If he didn't kiss me I was going to kill him.

His phone rang. He had the same ringtone as I did, which felt like a sign in the moment. He showed me Sloane's name on his screen before he answered. At first, we stayed locked in our too-close, magnet zone, but she must have said something serious because, suddenly, the spell was broken. Something in his eyes went from smiling to solemn, and he turned away from me to talk to her. When he got off the phone, he had to go.

He bought me a copy of *Sharp Objects* and told me to call him when I finished it. I intended to read the book faster than anyone had ever read it in history.

22

That afternoon in the bookstore replayed in my mind on a constant loop for the next three days. I would go to sleep swimming in a pool of Jason's eyes and would look forward to coming to in the morning, just so I could return to thinking about him. Every waking thought was pushed aside by his hands. That lovely raised vein in his forearm. The boyish way he acted when he was excited. How he seemed to like what I liked. The way he kept looking at me.

I finally had to draw a line in the sand with myself if I was ever going to get any work done. Luxuriating in thoughts of Jason all day and night was a mental extravagance I couldn't afford. This needed to be my psychological vacation spot instead of my permanent residence.

I sighed and gradually coerced myself back into the swing of things. I reluctantly reviewed my to-do list. The Sloane

Smythe launch was coming up in four days, and I was scheduled to start uploading some of the videos in advance.

I turned on my filming lights, gave myself a shake and pressed Record.

I decided to shoot the product close-ups first while they were still pristine and unused. I shot them against a white background with a bright light, creating a strong, almost-purple shadow. It looked very "high-fashion editorial" to me, which I liked.

I went on to film myself swatching and applying the eye shadows for the first of many swatch-and-review videos. Inspired by the edgy feel of the product shots, I created a hip, runway-inspired look for the first video.

I was feeling loose and relaxed, and witty ways of describing textures and colors were coming to mind easily as I filmed. I knew not to take this for granted, so I shot three videos back-to-back: one each for the eye shadow palettes, the blushes and the highlighters.

When I watched the footage, I was encouraged by how at ease with myself I seemed to be. I was clearly being genuine as I gave my opinion about the pros and cons of the products, and it made me realize that when I got back to the essence of why I loved making videos, all my cynical worries melted away.

I was growing excited about how the videos might turn out, so I poured myself a glass of wine and, despite the late hour, started editing. I found an otherworldly, ethereal beat to add to the swatch section and used a visually inventive music video for editing inspiration. I chose unique typefaces and spent an inordinate amount of time sizing and placing the type to hit the beat of the music.

Hours passed without my noticing. When I finally finished, I was so proud of the end result that I was eager to share one of the videos with someone. Perhaps the wine made me bold, but I decided to send one of them to Sloane as a preview of how hot shit my videos were shaping up to be. Sure, I was showing off a little, and maybe I was being a bit competitive with the fair- and dark-skinned YouTubers Sloane Smythe Cosmetics had also partnered with. *Whatever.* I entered the subject "Want a sneak peek?" in an email to Sloane, attached my video and sent it off.

I was asleep as soon as my head hit the pillow at 3:00 a.m.

23

When I groggily reached for my phone the next morning, there was already a response from Sloane. Eager to hear the praise I was expecting, I opened it immediately.

Ashley,

I've reviewed your video and am very concerned. The edginess of the editing and the makeup look you've chosen to create do not communicate the brand feel that we're after. I've shared it with Samantha, and she agrees that it is not acceptable. Can you please come meet with us today at 10:00 a.m. to discuss?

Sloane Smythe
CEO, Sloane Smythe Cosmetics

My face grew hot, and my heart rate had doubled by the time I finished reading the email. I felt like I was ten years old and being chastised by my teacher for not following instructions. "Yes, ma'am" was the only thing that came to my mind to say.

I agreed to the ten o'clock meeting.

* * *

Sunlight streamed into the Sloane Smythe Cosmetics boardroom despite the dour faces across the table from me.

"So, Ashley, as I'm sure you could tell by my email, I'm discouraged by the direction of the video so far. I know it's just a rough draft, but even in its early stage, I find it very disappointing," Sloane said to start the meeting.

I decided not to mention that it was, in fact, the finished product, not a draft.

"I thought it had a lot of energy," Jason offered in my defense. My skin tingled in response.

"The wrong kind of energy," said Sam in her whiney, judgy drawl. Her inflection sounded like a sonic eye roll.

"I agree," shot Sloane in her decisive, agitated way. "I don't remember discussing the unorthodox approach you took. And your delivery is very flat. The video is all edgy editing and no actual enthusiasm for the product."

She looked at me incredulously as if willing me to agree with her. "It won't sell," she then said matter-of-factly before I had a chance to say anything. She paused to think. The irises of her eyes were moving so quickly they seemed to be vibrating.

"We can't afford to make mistakes with this launch. My reputation is on the line, and if we don't sell at least as well as Charlotte Tilbury out of the gate, we won't get the distribution we need. All this investment will be out the window," she said, gesturing behind her, presumably at the large office and expensive boardroom furniture. "This would be a failure. And I don't do failure." Sloane half-closed her eyes and cocked her head.

"Of course not, Sloane. We won't let that happen," Sam said, somehow managing to sound reassuring to Sloane and condescending to me simultaneously.

"I think you're both overreacting," said Jason. "The video should have the personality of the channel, not the brand—"

"Oh, don't be defensive Jason," snapped Sam, cutting him off. "Just because this YouTube strategy was your idea doesn't mean you have to justify it if it's not working. You knew there were risks."

Sloane jumped in before Jason could respond. "I think our time would be better spent discussing the revisions we need so Ashley can reshoot."

Reshoot? I should have known this was where they were headed, but I was taken aback nonetheless. This was *my* channel. Could they make me do this? I vaguely remembered something in the papers I'd signed saying videos were "subject to the approval of Sloane Smythe Cosmetics." *Shit.*

"Ashley," Sam said, reading my mind, "don't worry, we all have a lot of experience with marketing, and we know what will sell. Your commission is very generous, so it's in your best interest to work *with* us."

I was feeling overwhelmed and wasn't sure what to do. I decided to take notes and process everything later when I wasn't feeling so put on the spot.

I filled page after page of my notebook as the discussion continued and sank deeper and deeper into my chair.

When the meeting finally ended, Jason walked me out. I was shell-shocked and frankly not relishing the fact that he'd just witnessed my belittling at the hands of Sloane and Sam.

"Hey, are you okay?" he asked, looking concerned.

"Yeah, of course," I said, shrugging, determined to come off as strong and low-maintenance around him. "It's not a big deal," I lied, secretly savoring his concern.

"I'm glad you're taking all this so well. Y'know, I could help you. If you need a sounding board or a second opinion, we could talk through stuff . . ." He trailed off.

"Oh? You and Sam would be happy to meet up?" I said

sweetly with only a hint of snarkiness. I shouldn't have. But I couldn't help myself.

"Look, I'm sorry about that. She came by my office when I was on the phone with you and insisted on coming." He seemed genuinely sorry.

"Oh." I averted my eyes and tried unsuccessfully not to smile. "Well maybe, then. I'll see you later," I said, looking up, allowing myself to meet his gaze as I walked into the elevator. He held it until the doors closed.

* * *

I walked home, desperately needing to be on my own to figure out what I thought about everything that had been said. The problem was, I had no idea what to think.

I was hurt and insulted that they didn't love the video that I had labored over and was so proud of. I mourned all the time I'd spent creatively shooting the products that they now wanted shot in a completely different way. I felt wounded that they didn't like "my delivery" in the video, which, to my ears, translated as they didn't like *me*.

I vacillated between flashes of anger and the need to lick my wounds for ten long blocks before I forced myself to consider the impossible.

Okay, what if they're right? I contemplated uncomfortably.

What if these changes will make the video more appealing to more people? That's not a bad thing. Maybe I should be more upbeat and enthusiastic in my videos as a rule. Other successful YouTubers are, I thought, starting to talk myself into it.

"It's business. It's not personal," I said quietly, pushing myself over the edge while furiously trying to knit myself a thicker skin.

By the time I got home, I had resolved to give all their various "notes" a shot. I dropped my bag and went straight to my camera to set up for shooting a new video.

24

I watched take after take of myself on my computer screen.
I was bubbly, I was excited and I was obsessed with the new
Sloane Smythe line. I could hardly contain my enthusiasm. I
was practically freaking out.

Sloane and Sam were going to love it.

I reshot all the products bathed in natural light and edited
them with slow fades and clear, easy-to-read type. I was
wearing the makeup in a natural yet glam way that read well on
camera.

I edited everything to a jazzy, modern track.

When I was finally finished, I was exhausted. Taking other
people's opinions into consideration when putting together a
video seemed to take ten times more effort. The finished
product was very appealing: polished, sophisticated,
enthusiastic and warm. It was the polar opposite of my raw,

edgy, straight-talking original video.

I decided to ask Jason for his opinion. It wasn't just an excuse to be in contact with him, even though that was clearly part of it (who am I kidding?). I really did want to know what he thought, both professionally and personally, since this more conservative approach was a departure for me. He was the creative director, and I needed creative direction—or, perhaps more truthfully, creative validation.

I spent far too much time writing and rewriting my email to him until I finally erased everything and just went with this:

> *Hi Jason,*
>
> *New vid. What do you think?*
> *Almost finished* Sharp Objects. *LOVING.*
>
> *Ash*

I attached the video and sent it off, immediately second-guessing my use of the word *loving*.

I was shocked to get an immediate response. His email said:

> *Looking at it now . . . I knew you'd like* Sharp Objects.

Phew. No harm done. I counted down the twenty minutes it

would take for him to watch the whole video.

Practically on cue, his name appeared in my inbox. I clicked.

I think Sloane and Sam will be really happy. Good job.

I nodded with my whole torso, agreeing with his assessment.

But what do YOU think?

Five excruciating minutes passed before he replied.

I think it doesn't quite seem like you. Listen, I'm going to share it with Sloane. Will get back to you soon.

I stared at my inbox, waiting impatiently. I refreshed my screen every few minutes, just in case. After ten minutes of nothing, I clicked over to Sephora and filled a basket with no intention of checking out, just to pass the time.

At last, the email came in.

"Big hit" was all it said.

25

Launch day finally arrived. I published the video at 7:00 a.m. as promised, even though it was not my usual upload day.

My phone pinged. It was a text from Jason.

Free for lunch?

My heart—the predictable thing that it is—started pounding.

Little early don't you think? I sassed.

I meant later!

Sure.

Will call you.

I grinned to myself, unable to be cool. Possible outfits started running through my head as my heart continued to thump.

I looked back at my computer screen.

My "New Sloane Smythe Cosmetics Eye Shadows | Medium Skin Tone | Review & Swatches" video had been up for fifteen minutes and already had 12,868 views. I took a peek at the comments. A few "thanks for the review" type messages and some requests for comparison videos were coming in.

Comparison video—that's a good idea, I thought to myself, considering which high-end brand I'd compare Sloane Smythe products to. *Tom Ford maybe? Probably Burberry since I have all the products already.* I jotted down some notes.

As I flipped the page in my notebook, I noticed a new comment come in.

Another sellout was all it said.

I inhaled sharply, and my eyes widened. I clicked on the commenter's username, "TheRealAmanda" to see who she was. Her channel page didn't have a photo, like many viewers who don't make videos themselves. A little snooping on her page revealed that she was subscribed mainly to smaller beauty gurus with subscribers in the thousands, not millions.

I clicked back to the comments. By now, twenty people had replied to TheRealAmanda's comment and more were piling on.

Yeah, I was thinking the same thing. This is totally sponsored, said Emily Hammonds.

Takin' the money. Just another beauty channel that's turned into a giant ad, said Brittney O.

The fame has gone to her head. She thinks she can just do paid videos and we won't notice? Does she think we're stupid? said Juicyjuice.

Her makeup looks so basic bitch, said Katykatekate.

I can't believe how fake she is in this, said TheLeAnnRhimes.

She's changed. I used to love how real she was. Now she sounds like all the rest, said CuteBiscuit.

Drinking game: Take a shot every time she says EXCITED! said Jackie Brooks.

No integrity!!!!! said Suzy B.

I've got some frosting for all that cake on your face, said GameBoy9118.

I flinched. *Oh my god, gamers are disgusting.* Feeling nauseous, I closed my laptop.

26

"Is something the matter?" Jason asked when I called to cancel lunch.

I wasn't sure what to tell him. It was too early to know if I could trust him, although there'd been some promising signs. Even if I could trust Jason, he worked for Sloane, so he'd be obliged to tell her that my video was bombing and that the comments had blown up into an all-out hate attack. I was debating taking the video down.

"No, I'm just worried about the video," I said in the understatement of the century.

"Why? I heard it's doing really well."

I paused, unsure what he was talking about. "Hmm?" I mumbled incoherently.

"Sales are going through the roof. And most of the clicks are from your video. You're a star around here," he said.

"What? I mean, really?" I fumbled for what to say.

"Yeah, Sloane and Sam want to increase your video schedule this month. Sloane's going to message you to set up a meeting."

"Oh. R-right, sure," I stammered, needing to get off the phone to properly process this bizarre information. I asked for a rain check for lunch, mumbled some more and hung up.

"What the fucking hell?" I said to myself incredulously.

My phone pinged. It was a text from Chels. I cringed guiltily.

I'd been avoiding Chels for weeks now as a way of avoiding the truth. Choosing to see her would have been tantamount to choosing to tell her about everything that was going on, and I had been too chicken shit for that.

I just heard FROM SOMEONE ELSE that you quit your job??? WTF?

One glance back at the comments section of my video confirmed my fear that the negative comments hadn't abated. In fact, they'd escalated to vicious name-calling, hate-mongering accusations and worse.

OMFG who the fuck does she think she is? Stop the cunty sponsored shit! She's exactly what's wrong with YouTube and needs to be deceased, commented 09jess8921.

I'm coming over, was my text back to Chels.

27

I told Chels everything.

I confessed to hiding my obsession with makeup from her. I told her about starting my YouTube channel in secret five months ago. I described what it was like being a shy exhibitionist, a flesh-and-blood oxymoron—too anxious about being judged to expose my heart to people in my life but somehow happy to display it for all to see on the Internet. I explained why I loved making videos and how nourishing my interactions with other beauty addicts felt. How the support of these women was helping me feel that the real me could actually be loveable.

Then I told her about that crazy morning two months ago now that I still didn't have an explanation for. I told her about the check from Google, and I didn't stop talking when her chin hit the ground. I told her how all my new subscribers suddenly gave me clout with brands. How I was considered a top "influencer" now. I told her about the boxes and boxes of makeup that were being sent to me every week in hopes of a mention to my "audience." I told her about the things brands were now offering—trips to Hawaii, Turks and Caicos, and New York, among other things, as an incentive to talk about their products. I told her about quitting my job. I told her about Sloane Smythe Cosmetics. I told her how shitty it felt to make videos where I wasn't being true to myself. How letting Sloane Smythe control my videos made me feel like I was betraying my viewers and, most of all, myself. How all those haters were probably right; I had no integrity.

"Jesus" was all Chels could say for several minutes.

I let her digest it all. Then I said, "What do you think?" I dreaded the answer but needed her advice.

"Well, I think you have a decision to make."

28

I pushed open the frosted-glass door to the Sloane Smythe offices and self-consciously smiled at Sabrina, the receptionist. I imagined people here had seen the video, but I wasn't sure if they'd read the comments.

Sabrina smiled back warmly.

"Hi, sweetheart, congratulations."

I didn't know what to say since I didn't know what she was talking about.

Before I could ask, Sloane strode into the reception area.

"There she is!" she said with a gregarious chuckle. Her voice was almost unbearably sunny and friendly. Then she started doing the strangest thing. She started clapping.

And, one by one, others in the office followed suit. Before I knew it, everyone was standing and clapping. I noticed Sam standing near the boardroom, first adjusting her hair and then distractedly slapping her stationary left hand with her right. Jen was beside her smiling genuinely, doing a cute, fast-paced "happy clap." And in the far corner was Jason, wearing a dimpled smile on his face and clapping his cupped, strong hands.

I'd dreamt of moments like this. Except, in my dreams, I was being applauded for something I was proud of.

Embarrassed, I begged for everyone to stop and sheepishly followed Sloane into the boardroom where Jen, Sam and Jason were filing in ahead of us.

"Your video is averaging six hundred sale conversions an hour. You've just made close to $60,000 in twenty-four hours," Sloane said smoothly.

I gulped. I tried to calculate in my head what that likely meant for her, only to come up with "a lot more than that."

"The launch is going very well, and your video is outselling the 'fair' and 'dark' videos by a huge margin," Sloane continued, beaming.

"We've been brainstorming ways to leverage your success," she said in her abrupt way that put me on edge. She went to the easel-sized flip chart in the corner of the room. My name was scrawled in green marker at the top of the page and there were notes scribbled in red underneath it.

She flipped the large page over in a quick, full-body motion that mimicked her staccato way of speaking. The page she revealed had the headline "Brand Activation" in green and several red bullet points underneath.

"We'd like to plan some events for you to attend. We're thinking an appearance at our booth at IMATS, maybe a few meet-ups with your fans in LA and New York where you show them the line in person. And we'd like to increase your video schedule to two a week from now on," she said, glancing at the schedule that Sam had passed her. "You can start with a tutorial on concealing imperfections using my color-correcting mousse concealer…" She trailed off, scowling at the schedule.

In a soft voice, I said, "I'm sorry. I can't do that."

The room went silent as all heads turned to me.

"What did you say?" asked Sloane.

"I said I can't do any more videos for you." I was looking at the table. With my head still down, I lifted my eyes to see the shocked faces across from me. Jason's startled look was beginning to morph into a bemused smirk.

"Uh, what are you talking about," said Sam in her condescending whine. "You agreed to a partnership to create videos—"

"I'm planning to take down the current video, and you can keep the commission," I interjected, slowly and intentionally, before she could finish.

"You're planning to what?" Sloane suddenly roared. "Oh, nuh-nuh-nuh-nuh-nuh-nuh-no," was her sing-song, rapid-fire response. "You won't be doing that. You would be in breach of our agreement. You need my authorization to stray in any way from the schedule we agreed on," she said matter-of-factly with a caustic smile.

"I don't care," I said calmly, looking away from her enraged blue eyes.

"I'll sue, you little piece of shit!" Sloane yelled, startling me. "Who do you think you are? Do you have any idea what you're doing right now?" She spoke with such piercing intensity I felt like I'd been hit. In a quieter, dismissive voice, she added, "You're just a fearful girl with nothing of substance to say. You talk about makeup in your tiny apartment. That's all."

A moment passed, and when I didn't take back what I said, she lost it, her mid-Atlantic accent flaring as she spat, "I'm giving you an opportunity of a lifetime. Don't be stee-uw-pid and throw this all away."

My stomach tightened into knots. I felt shame creeping over me, making every inch of my body feel defective. Whenever it was pointed out that I wasn't the vivacious, fascinating and strong woman I so wanted to be, I would predictably spiral down the drain of shame, humiliated by who I actually was. I guess my parents' attempt to raise me to be a charismatic leader backfired.

I looked over at Jason, mortified that he was witnessing this. But the look on his face wasn't of pity or disgust. His eyebrows showed concern, but his eyes were soft. His mouth parted as if he were about to say something, but he smiled encouragingly instead. He was supporting me. He could *see* me, and for some reason, he believed in me. I felt a surge of energy.

"You're right, Sloane. I am a fearful girl who talks about makeup in my little apartment. And you're right. I'm not saving the world." I paused, feeling a thrumming in my veins. "But before your 'opportunity,' at least I was being honest. At least I was being creative and growing as a person. At least I was being true to myself. Those are the reasons I started my channel. Not to make money. So, you see, this 'opportunity' you've given me? It's not for me. It's taking my channel in the wrong direction. For *my* brand."

I reached for my purse, got up quietly and left the room before anyone could say anything.

As soon as I was past the boardroom's threshold, I sped up and knew better than to look back.

"Ashley, wait!" I heard Jason say behind me just as I reached the front door.

I turned to see him jogging toward me.

"You were amazing in there," he said looking at me in a funny way. "They think I'm out here trying to change your mind, so shake your head before you leave."

I smiled conspiratorially.

"Meet me for a drink later," he said under his breath so no one around us could hear.

I smiled and then shook my head. And just as the door was closing behind me, I gave him a wink.

29

So? came Chels' text not five minutes into the best walk home of my life.

I told her I'm taking down the video, and they can keep the commission.

How much was the commission? Good ol' Chels.

$58,320, I texted back.

Holy shit.

I know. I'm doing the right thing, right?

What do you think?

I looked around me. Everything seemed to be moving in slow motion. I saw a group of women, around my age, shopping together, laughing. There were women in their forties getting their hair dyed in the salon across the street. A group of teenaged girls passed me, walking home from school, some already wearing makeup. And as I walked past a storefront with a floor-to-ceiling glass window, I looked at my reflection. What I saw gave me my answer.

I was looking at a woman who had finally crossed an elusive line in her mind. For the first time in my life, I felt that I was worth something. I felt that I was enough.

* * *

I walked into my apartment, went directly to my camera, turned on the power and pressed Record.

When I finished talking thirty-seven minutes later, I uploaded the video with no editing, no music and no type. I titled it "Why I'm Taking Down My Channel."

One Year Later

30

There's no point for me to go into too much detail about what I said in the first part of that video. I just explain what happened and you already know all about that. But the more I talked, the more I needed to talk. The more I needed to explain.

"I'm starting fresh. With no sponsorships, no free products, no free trips, no brand partnerships, no endorsements, no affiliate links, nothing. The same as it was in the beginning. I don't want a channel that's about selling things. I don't want a channel where what I say is influenced by a commission check or a free trip to Bora Bora. I only want to be true to myself and honest with you," I said.

Although more than a few people thought I was insane at the time, I'd never felt surer of anything in my life. I had jumped into this bizarre world of YouTube fame and come out the other end in such a concentrated way that the experience had given me the gift of certainty.

When I had started making videos, I was a free agent with dreams of growing my channel. I didn't know it at the time, but what I was dreaming of becoming was an entrepreneur. But once the reality of having a channel with the demands of a successful small business kicked in, I discovered that I was on a slope that wasn't just slippery—it was covered in an extra layer of dimethicone. Let me explain.

Businesses by definition are concerned about the bottom line. Monetizing your content is just what you have to do to make your business viable. But even the most harmless-seeming methods of creating income from your channel have an insidious way of changing what you put out there. Even affiliate links—clickable hyperlinks to products mentioned in videos that pay a commission if the product is purchased—started to make me uneasy after a while. Everyone uses them, and they're just a passive form of income, right? But when viewed through a business lens, it would soon make the most sense to feature *only* the brands that kicked back. Maybe a small brand would get thrown in every once in a while to "keep things real," but, for the most part, the better business decision would become the rule. It had never occurred to me why certain brands seemed to get all the love on YouTube, but now I knew.

I believe makeup is a true egalitarian art form, one that every woman, for the most part, can and does take part in. We all need a creative outlet, and makeup is it for so many of us. When we transform ourselves from tired to cute, we transform how we feel—and that's an empowering thing. But if we let the business of beauty take over our community, I think we'll have lost something important. Makeup companies with their own gigantic bottom lines dictating their actions shouldn't be the ones controlling our passion. I think we need to take back our power.

Demand for makeup is booming globally. It's big business with billions in rising profits, and YouTube has had a huge part to play in that. The more beauty YouTubers participate in fueling that fire in women, the more need there is for unbiased points of view. It's not fair otherwise.

I'm not naïve. I understand the way the world works. I'm not against brands advertising or YouTubers making a living. I get it. But does it all have to be at the expense of what made YouTube great to begin with? Does the tidal wave of commercialism have to drown the soul of why we're all here in the first place?

Integrity can come in degrees, but I've discovered I prefer the all-or-nothing variety. If I were to compare my channel content to journalism, I'd rather be *The New York Times* of beauty than the *National Enquirer*. While some will have no problem letting brands influence content, I've come to believe it should be church and state. I will allow ads to appear on my channel, but I refuse to be an advertorial.

Successful vloggers and bloggers are considered "influencers" now, but on behalf of whom? If it's not our viewers, there's something very wrong.

As I said in that infamous video, "I've debated whether to just take down the videos I'm not proud of and continue on this channel with a new path or to take this channel down and start a new one. The better business decision would be the former. But I've decided that the only way to start from a truly honest place is the latter. I want every subscriber to have voluntarily clicked the Subscribe button, and I want every video on the channel to have come from a pure place.

"So. I'm starting a new channel. Every product I feature there will be bought by me. I will not be communicating with brands except to reject any offers from them. Everything I say and show will be completely impartial and unbiased. It's just what I need to do to stay true to me. And it's how I plan to prove that just because I'm interested in makeup, it doesn't mean I'm not an intelligent woman with integrity who wants to make a meaningful contribution. If you're into that, my new channel is called 'The Old Ash.' It's linked below. Bye."

Crazy, huh?

What's even more bananas is the video spread at light speed

across the Internet. And my new channel, I'm happy to report, has just today passed four million subscribers. That's a lot fewer than nine million, but, as you've probably figured by now, it's not just about the numbers for me.

I'm able to live very comfortably off my YouTube earnings and have not had to call my old boss back. But I'm okay if I have to someday. I really am.

I have a budget that I put aside every month to buy new products for review and to use in tutorials. I now have a form rejection letter that I send to brands whenever they contact me. And many of them still do, surprisingly.

I shared my new channel with my parents not long after I started it. And while they thought it was peculiar at first, my mom now asks me for makeup recommendations. I've also "come out" as a beauty junkie to all my friends and stopped trying to hide that part of me. It's funny, but when I finally stopped being afraid of being judged, it rarely happened. I got nothing but love and maybe a few bewildered remarks from guys.

Chels started a YouTube channel of her own about being a single woman, and it's doing really well. I'm going over to her place to film a collab video later today.

Sloane Smythe Cosmetics never did sue me as they'd threatened to. By taking down my channel, I suppose I diminished the damages they could ask for in a suit. But that's not why I did it, and I only reasoned that out after the fact. Ultimately, there wasn't enough blood to be had from this stone, I reckon. I heard they found another beauty guru with millions of subscribers to replace me, but, for whatever reason, their sales never really took off. You can still get Sloane's products online, but they're not sold at Barneys and Neiman Marcus the way she had planned. I heard they moved to smaller offices across town.

And Jason? He stopped working with Sloane a few weeks after that crazy meeting. He decided to take a year off to film a documentary about YouTube stars, if you can believe it. He's at Sundance this week to promote it.

And me? I'll be flying to Park City tomorrow for the premiere. Because not only do I star in the film, I also happen to be the director's girlfriend.

Coming soon by Harlow Miller:

Sticky Gloss, a novella.

Ash and Jason embark on two exhilarating new adventures: one filming a documentary about up-and-coming YouTube stars, and another between themselves.

Follow Harlow Miller on Facebook and @harlowmillerauthor on Instagram to be notified when *Sticky Gloss* launches.

ABOUT THE AUTHOR

Harlow Miller lives in the Pacific Northwest with her husband and a dog she refuses to believe is already nine years old. *Cake Face* is her first work of fiction. She can be reached at harlowmiller@gmail.com.

Made in the USA
Charleston, SC
09 July 2016